www.capstonepub.com
Visit our website to find out more information about Heinemann-Raintree books.

To order:
☎ Phone 800-747-4992
💻 Visit www.capstonepub.com to browse our catalog and order online.

Edited by Daniel Nunn, Rebecca Rissman, and Sian Smith
Designed by Cynthia Della-Rovere
Picture research by Mica Brancic
Production by Victoria Fitzgerald
Originated by Capstone Global Library Ltd
Printed and bound in China by South China Printing Company Ltd

16 15 14 13 12
10 9 8 7 6 5 4 3 2 1

Library of Congress Cataloging-in-Publication Data
Nunn, Daniel.
  Numbers in Italian : I Numeri / Daniel Nunn.
    p. cm.—(World languages - Numbers)
  Includes bibliographical references and index.
  ISBN 978-1-4329-6676-8 (hb)—ISBN 978-1-4329-6683-6 (pb) 1. Italian language—Textbooks for foreign speakers—English—Juvenile literature. 2. Counting—Juvenile literature. I. Title.
  PC1129.E5N88 2012
  458.2'421—dc23   2011050550

Acknowledgments

We would like to thank Shutterstock for permission to reproduce photographs: © Agorohov, © Aleksandrs Poliscuks, © Alex James Bramwell, © Andreas Gradin, © Andrey Armyagov, © archidea, © Arogant, © atoss, © Baloncici, © Benjamin Mercer, © blackpixel, © charles taylor, © Chris Bradshaw, © cloki, © dcwcreations, © DenisNata, © Diana Taliun, © Eric Isselée, © Erik Lam, © Fatseyeva, © Feng Yu, © g215, © Hywit Dimyadi, © Iv Nikolny, © J. Waldron, © jgl247, © joingate, © karam Miri, © Karkas, © kedrov, © LittleMiss, © Ljupco Smokovski, © Lori Sparkia, © Max Krasnov, © Michelangelus, © Mike Flippo, © mimo, © Nordling, © Olga Popova, © Pavel Sazonov, © pics fine, © Rosery, © Ruth Black, © Shmel, © Stacy Barnett, © Steve Collender, © Suzanna, © Tania Zbrodko, © topseller, © Vasina Natalia, © Veniamin Kraskov, © Vinicius Tupinamba, © Volodymyr Krasyuk, © Vorm in Beeld, © Winston Link, © xpixel.

Cover photographs reproduced with permission of Shutterstock: number 1 (© Leigh Prather), number 2 (© Glovatskiy), number 3 (© Phuriphat). Back cover photograph of toy cars reproduced with permission of Shutterstock (© Vorm in Beeld, © Andreas Gradin, © charles taylor, © Benjamin Mercer, © Chris Bradshaw, © Nordling, © Arogant, © jgl247).

We would like to thank Nino Puma for his invaluable assistance in the preparation of this book.

Every effort has been made to contact copyright holders of material reproduced in this book. Any omissions will be rectified in subsequent printings if notice is given to the publisher.

Contents

Uno

un cane

C'è un cane.

un maglione

C'è un maglione.

Due

un gatto

Ci sono due gatti.

una scarpa

Ci sono due scarpe.

Tre

una ragazza

Ci sono tre ragazze.

una sedia

Ci sono tre sedie.

Quattro

un uccello

Ci sono quattro uccelli.

un cuscino

Ci sono quattro cuscini.

Cinque

un giocattolo

Ci sono cinque giocattoli.

un libro

Ci sono cinque libri.

Sei

un cappotto

Ci sono sei cappotti.

una matita

Ci sono sei matite.

Sette

una arancia

Ci sono sette arance.

un biscotto

Ci sono sette biscotti.

15

Otto

una macchina

Ci sono otto macchine.

un cappello

Ci sono otto cappelli.

Nove

un palloncino

Ci sono nove palloncini.

una candela

Ci sono nove candele.

Dieci

una mela

Ci sono dieci mele.

un fiore

Ci sono dieci fiori.

Dictionary

See words in the "How To Say It" columns for a rough guide to pronunciations.

Italian Word	How To Say It	English Word
arancia / arance	ar-ran-chah / ar-ran-cheh	orange / oranges
biscotto / biscotti	biss-cott-oh / biss-cott-ee	cookie / cookies
c'è	cheh	there is
candela / candele	kan-deh-lah / kan-deh-leh	candle / candles
cane	kann-eh	dog
cappello / cappelli	kap-ell-oh / kap-ell-ee	hat / hats
cappotto / cappotti	ka-pott-oh / ka-pott-ee	coat / coats
ci sono	chee sonn-oh	there are
cinque	chin-kway	five
cuscino / cuscini	koo-shee-no / koo-shee-nee	cushion / cushions
dieci	dee-eh-chee	ten
due	doo-eh	two
fiore / fiori	fee-o-reh / fee-o-ree	flower / flowers
gatto / gatti	gatt-oh / gatt-ee	cat / cats
giocattolo / giocattoli	jo-kat-tow-loh / jo-kat-tow-lee	toy / toys
libro / libri	lee-broh / lee-bree	book / books
macchina / macchine	mak-kina / mak-kin-eh	car / cars

Italian Word	How To Say It	English Word
maglione	mall-ee-own-eh	sweater
matita / matite	matt-ee-tah / matt-ee-teh	pencil / pencils
mela / mele	may-lar / may-leh	apple / apples
nove	no-veh	nine
otto	ot-toh	eight
palloncino / palloncini	pall-on-chee-noh / pall-on-chee-nee	balloon / balloons
quattro	qwa-troh	four
ragazza / ragazze	ragg-at-sa / ragg-at-seh	girl / girls
scarpa / scarpe	skarr-pah / skarr-peh	shoe / shoes
sedia / sedie	seh-dee-ah / seh-dee-eh	chair / chairs
sei	saee	six
sette	sett-eh	seven
tre	treh	three
uccello / uccelli	oo-chel-oh / oo-chel-ee	bird / birds
un / una	oo-n / oo-nah	a
un / una / uno	oo-n / oo-nah / oo-noh	one

Index

Notes for Parents and Teachers
In Italian, nouns are either masculine or feminine. The word for "a" or "one" changes accordingly—either un (masculine) or una (feminine). "Uno" is used when you write the number one on its own rather than as part of a sentence.